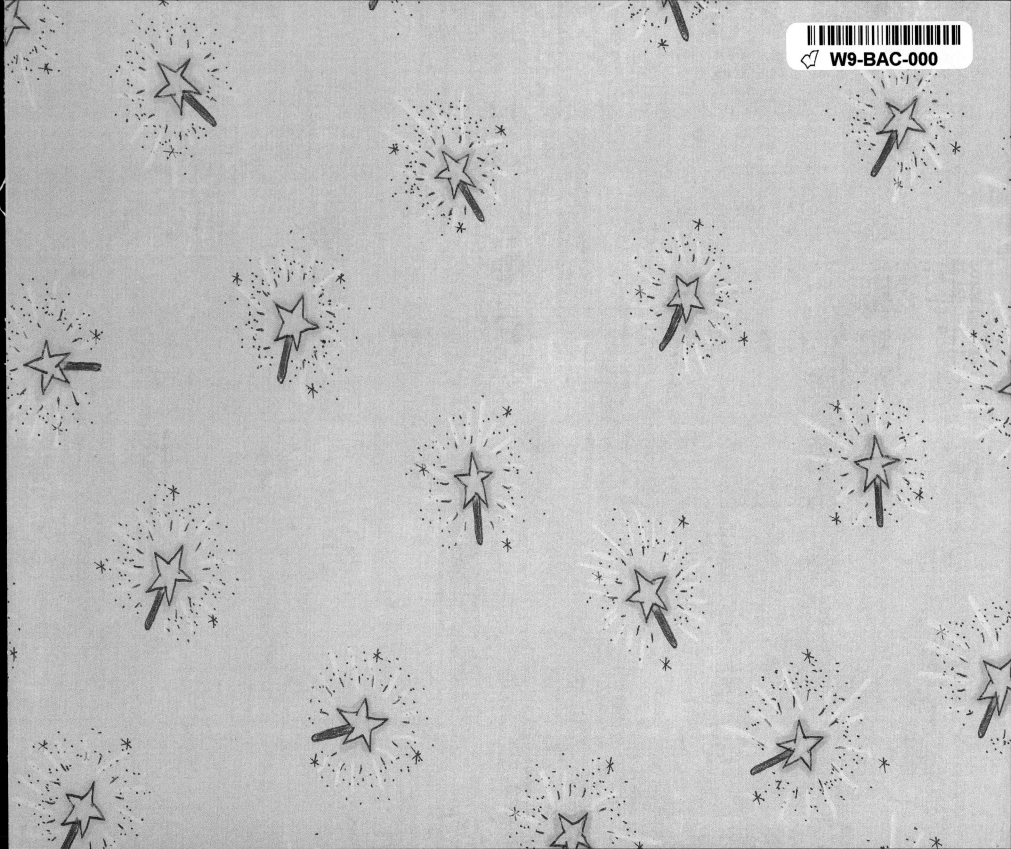

Requests for permission to make copies of any part of the work should be mailed to:
Tekita Enterprises
Franklin Corner Dental Assoc.
Permissions Department
96 Franklin Corner Road
Lawrenceville, NJ 08648
Terry@thewindowsillfairy.com
www.TheWindowsillFairy.com

Library of Congress Cataloging-in-Publication Data
Zimmerman, Terry 2011
The Windowsill Fairy / By Terry Zimmerman; Pictures by Kim Kost

Summary: The Windowsill Fairy lights up her magical wand that guides the Tooth Fairy to a child's newly lost tooth.

ISBN 978-0-578-13196-2

A big thank you to Paul Kost, David Nathanson, Gary Barbetta, and Jordan Zimmerman
for your time, dedication, endless hours, and commitment. Kudos to David for his creativity bringing this book and box to life!

The Windowsill FAIRY

A Tooth Fairy Tale

Written by Terry Zimmerman Illustrated by Kim Kost

This book is dedicated to all the children
who persevere through life's growing pains
with determination and might.
Good things happen to those who work hard.
Dreams are attainable.

This book belongs to:

_____

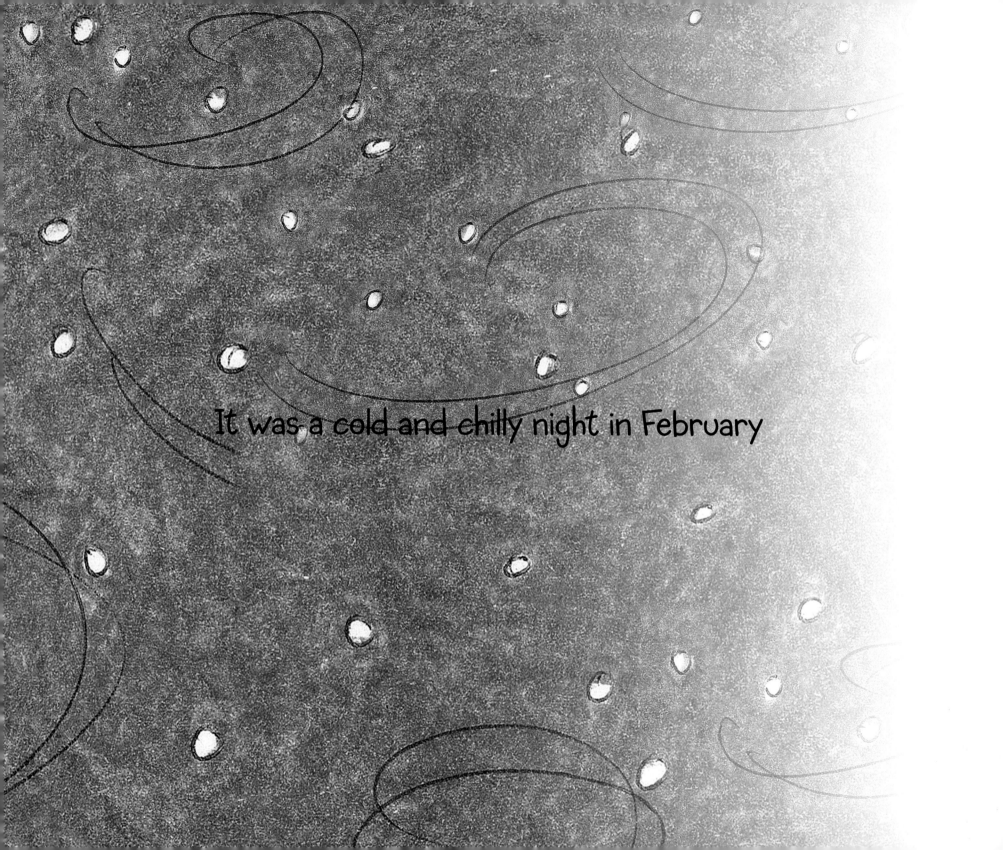

It was a cold and chilly night in February

when Rebecca Lee lost  her very first tooth.

That cute little tooth had been around for a very long time. Rebecca ate all sorts of healthy foods like carrots, apples, celery, and pears her whole life. That little tooth could crunch and munch with all its might. Suddenly, one day her tooth became loose!

It *wiggled.* It waggled. It WOBBLED.

It even flapped in the breeze. Rebecca was having trouble eating the apple that her mother packed in her lunchbox.

Many of her classmates were losing their teeth as well. Hannah's tooth fell out while she was jumping rope in gym class.

Jake's tooth fell out when he sneezed in science lab.

Derek lost his tooth while eating pizza in the cafeteria.

That night after dinner, Rebecca could not bear that wiggly little tooth any longer. She marched into the bathroom and plopped herself in front of the mirror. She was determined to pull out her tooth all by herself.

She twisted.
She yanked.
She even turned it sideways.

Finally, that silly little tooth popped out into the sink!

Rebecca was so excited. She screamed and hollered until her whole family, even her two little dogs, came running into the bathroom to find out what all the noise was about. Boy, did she look different!

The dogs barked with approval! After all the excitement that evening, it was time for bed. Rebecca had always been a curious little girl. She asked her mother and father, "How in the world will the Tooth Fairy know I lost my tooth tonight?" "How will she find my tooth?"

Rebecca's mother tucked her into bed, then brought a special box to Rebecca's bedside. Inside the box was Wanda, the Windowsill Fairy. Wanda was holding a pouch for Rebecca's tooth. Her father told her the tooth would be safe and sound in the pouch. Rebecca carefully put her tooth inside, tied the pouch tightly, and handed it to her Mom, who placed it on the windowsill. Her parents softly patted her head and kissed her goodnight.

Next, her father turned on the fairy's wand. With a flick of a switch, Rebecca's bedroom was glowing brilliantly in the night. The bright light would guide the Tooth Fairy straight to Rebecca's house, and even better, straight to her tooth on the windowsill. She closed her eyes and made a wish...

Back at the Tooth Fairy's castle, the snow was falling softly. A wicked snow storm was on its way. Flying in the snow could be very difficult and dangerous for a fairy. The wings of a fairy could easily freeze and stop fluttering. Rebecca would be disappointed if the Tooth Fairy could not make the trip.

The glowing signal coming from Rebecca's windowsill alerted the Tooth Fairy there was a newly lost tooth that needed to be picked up immediately. Not only was the tooth a baby tooth, but a beautiful, cavity free FRONT tooth. It was so clean and shiny. The Tooth Fairy suited up and headed out into the cold night. It was late and the snow was coming down quickly. With all her might and determination, she sped through the falling snowflakes, weaving in and out of them. She could not disappoint Rebecca.

As her journey was coming to an end, the light in the window guided the Tooth Fairy closer. She was getting tired and her wings were slowing down. She could hear Rebecca's wish over and over again in her head...

I wish with all my might that the Tooth Fairy comes tonight!

I wish with all my might that the Tooth Fairy comes tonight!

I wish with all my might that the Tooth Fairy comes tonight!

I wish with all my might that the Tooth Fairy comes tonight!

Just as the Tooth Fairy approached Rebecca's house, Wanda opened the bedroom window ever so slightly. The Tooth Fairy slipped in through the crack. Both fairies smiled at one another, then fluttered over to Rebecca, who was peacefully sleeping. In the blink of an eye, with the soft humming sound of the fluttering wings, the exchange was made.

The Tooth Fairy took the pearly white tooth and made Rebecca's wish come true. The dogs started to awaken, but before they could bark, the Tooth Fairy had vanished out the window.

When Rebecca woke up the next morning, she went straight to the pouch next to Wanda and hollered throughout the house, "Yes! It worked. It worked! My wish came true!" Looking inside the pouch, Rebecca saw exactly what she wished for last night.

Rebecca looked
at the Windowsill Fairy.
She winked and
blew her a kiss.

Top 10 Things to
Keep Your Teeth Healthy

1. Brush all your teeth for two minutes morning and night.

2. Brush your tongue to remove germs.

3. Rinse your mouth for 30 seconds after brushing.

4. Floss your teeth once a day.

5. Change your toothbrush every three months.

6. Visit the dentist two times a year.

7. Limit sugary snacks and drinks.

8. Eat healthy snacks like vegetables,
   low fat cheese, and yogurt.

9. Brush your teeth after sweets and treats.

10. Drink lots of water.

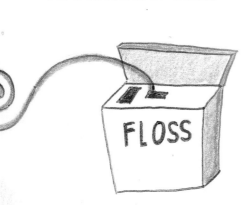

FLOSS

I lost my tooth...

Upper Teeth

A _____

B _____

C _____

D _____

E _____

F _____

G _____

H _____

I _____

J _____

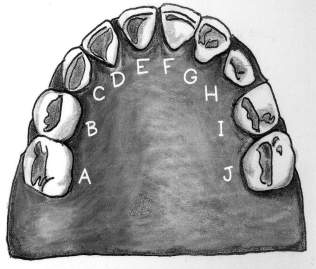

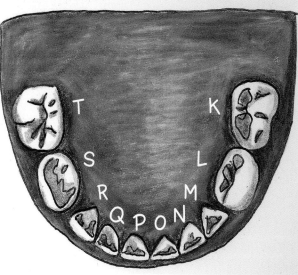

K _____

L _____

M _____

N _____

O _____

P _____

Q _____

R _____

S _____

T _____

Lower Teeth

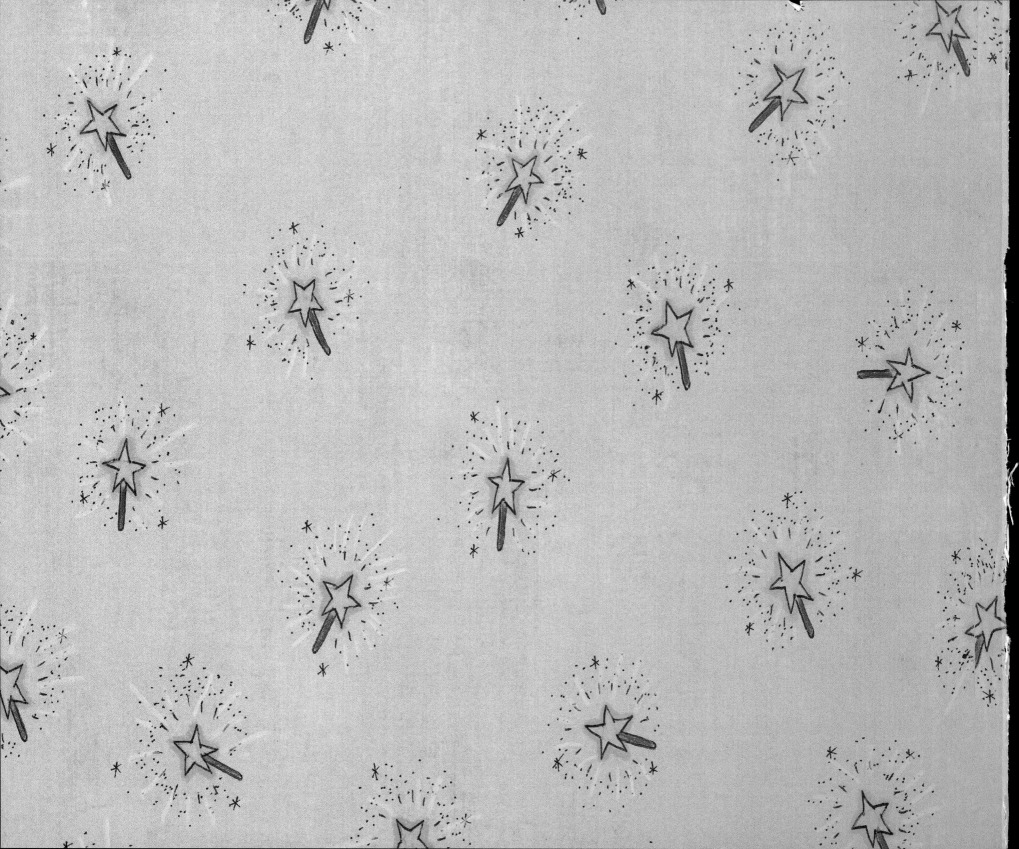